Chapters

by Kay Livorse
illustrated by Robert Casilla

Orlando   Boston   Dallas   Chicago   San Diego

Visit *The Learning Site!*

www.harcourtschool.com

Play Camps

In a Cheyenne village, boys and girls learned many skills at "play camp." For example, children learned to ride horses at an early age. Horses played an important role in the life of the Cheyenne.

Little Fox had been placed on a horse soon after he learned to walk. By age ten, he was an excellent rider and had his own pony. He was very comfortable riding his horse.

Little Fox and other boys his age also hunted small game with bows and arrows. They learned to approach the animals very quietly so they wouldn't frighten them away. When the boys were about thirteen, they were allowed to go hunting with the men.

Cheyenne mothers built small tipis for their daughters, and the girls did everything their mothers did. The women of the tribe took care of the household chores, which included setting up and taking down the tipis. They also gathered food and firewood.

After a hunt, the women cleaned and tanned the hides of the animals. When hides were tanned, the leather was made soft and the women made robes, moccasins, and other clothes for the family. They also made household equipment out of the bones and horns of the animals. The girls gathered berries and dried food to last through the winter.

Cheyenne girls and boys continued to learn through play. The children became more confident as their skills improved.

4

Mysterious Dogs

"Why do we call the horses 'mysterious dogs'?" Little Fox asked his grandfather, White Cloud.

"Before the horse came to us long ago, our dogs did much of the work that our horses do now," White Cloud answered.

Little Fox laughed and said, "You mean men rode the dogs on a buffalo hunt?"

"No, no," said White Cloud, laughing with his grandson. "The dogs would pull the travois. Now the horse does the work and can carry a heavier load."

"Tell me about the horses, Grandfather," said Little Fox.

"I can tell you what my grandfather told me and what his grandfather told him," said White Cloud. "Long ago, the Cheyenne lived along the rivers. They lived in lodges made of wood. The lodges were covered with earth and were very large."

"Grandfather, how could the tribe follow the buffalo?" said the boy. "They couldn't take their lodges with them like they do the tipi."

"You are exactly right, Little Fox. Our people's life was different then. We did not travel as much as we do now. We did not move the wood lodges. When we started using horses, we began to follow the buffalo herd.

"The tipi became our only home. We were able to move it easily when we had the help of the horse," said White Cloud.

"We had to change our life in many ways. Our pottery would break because we moved so much. Women had to make utensils from buffalo bone and horn, which did not break so easily."

7

White Cloud continued. "Before we had horses, we stayed in one place and tended to the crops we grew. We used tipis when we traveled, but that was not often. Now our people move several times a year.

"Once we learned to handle the horses, they made our lives easier. They helped us to become mighty hunters. The horse became important to us. Sometimes other tribes would try to capture our horses and ride away with them. We had to protect our hunting grounds, too."

Little Fox said, "If another tribe tried to use our territory, we used horses to chase them away, right Grandfather?"

"That is correct, Little Fox," White Cloud answered.

"Horses are so strong and fast," said Little Fox. "I think they are wonderful."

"Yes, they are," said White Cloud. "Horses have helped us to hunt together, too. We do not hunt buffalo alone. A single hunter might frighten the buffalo herd. He might get stampeded by them. Our hunt leaders make sure that everyone obeys the rules."

"Why did we become warriors, Grandfather?" asked Little Fox.

"When we traveled here, we had to defend our people. Settlers and other tribes wanted the land we lived on," said White Cloud.

"When I get bigger, I will become a leader. I am getting better with my bow. I am one of the best of my age on my pony," said Little Fox.

"It is good that you are confident, grandson, but you still have much to learn," said White Cloud in a firm voice.

Children's Games

"It's time for me to take my turn herding the horses, Grandfather. I'll have to hurry or I'll be late for my appointment," said Little Fox, laughing.

Little Fox's pinto was white with brown spots on it. He had named the horse Wind Runner. The animal was easy to train, and Little Fox knew his father and grandfather were pleased with the progress of both of them.

Little Fox and Wind Runner were a good team. They kept the horses from straying.

Little Fox and two of his friends caught some fish in a nearby stream. Little Fox took the fish home to his mother, who added them to the stew she was making.

Laughing Water, his older sister, was learning to work with porcupine quills. Her embroidery was very beautiful. Little Fox treasured the moccasins that she made for him.

"Some of us are going to play hunting buffalo. Come with us, Laughing Water," said Little Fox. "You can do the quillwork later."

With her mother's permission, Laughing Water left to join the others. On the way, she put a piece of cactus on a stick to stand for the buffalo. She gave it to one of the boys, and he pretended to graze like a buffalo.

The rest of the boys pretended to mount horses and surround the buffalo. If they managed to hit the buffalo with their weapons, the buffalo was defeated. If they missed, the buffalo would try and catch them.

The children celebrated a victory when they won against the buffalo.

As they brought the buffalo back to the play camp, the girls cried out for help as if their camp was being invaded.

The boys fought off the invaders. The girls quickly dismantled the tipis and tied them to their dogs, which the girls protected as if they were horses. They ran away with their dogs running behind them.

The girls hid from everyone until the fight was over. Then the boys found the girls, and they all returned to camp.

When they returned to their mother, they found her making pemmican for their next move. They would leave soon because the buffalo had moved away.

Little Fox left to tend to the horse herd again. He would move them to a new pasture. They also needed food for the journey.

Laughing Water stayed with her mother to help make pemmican. Dried berries and dried buffalo meat were mixed with fat. These were the basic ingredients. Sometimes they added berries, nuts, or cornmeal.

After the next hunt, the tribe traveled to meet many other tribes for the annual Sun Dance. It was the most sacred of all rituals.

The program lasted for eight days in the special Sun Dance Lodge that many would help build. There was dancing for four days and nights, and prayers and offerings were given.

After proving their courage through the Sun Dance, the warriors believed that their prayers would be answered.

Their horses would carry them.